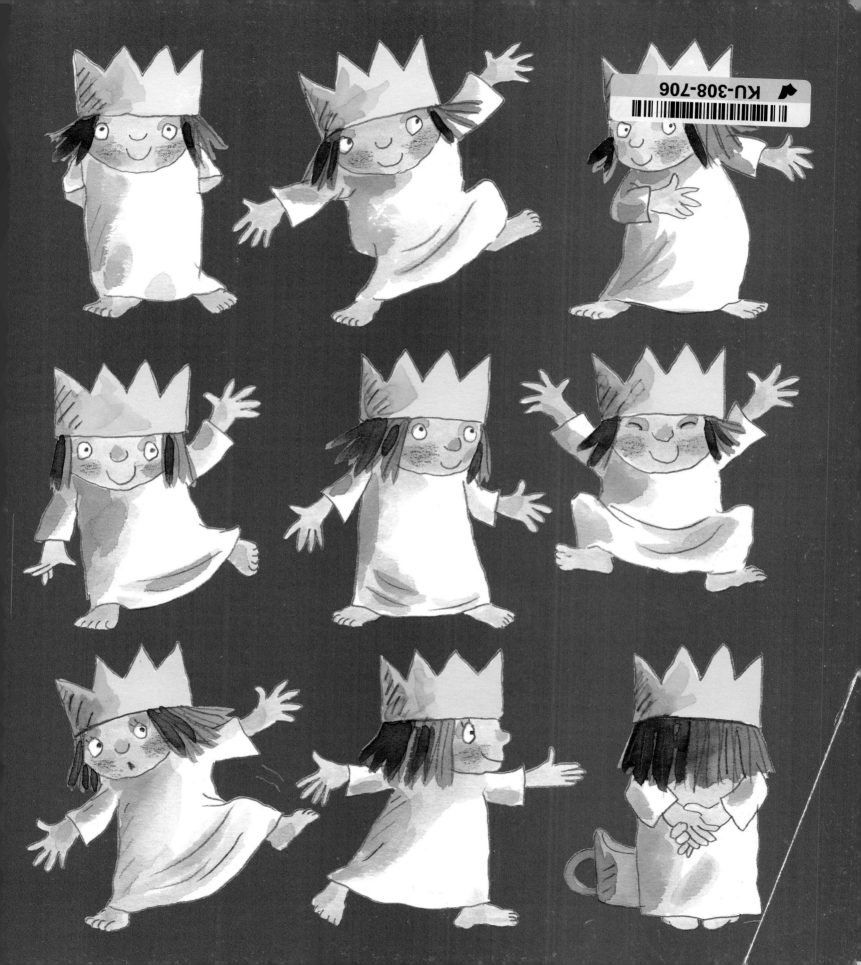

With my thanks to
San Kiu Lieu and Samantha Riches
who gave me the idea for this story and their
permission to use it when they were at
Keyworth Primary School in London.

This paperback edition first published in 2009 by Andersen Press Ltd.

First published in Great Britain in 1999 by Andersen Press Ltd., 20 Vauxhall Bridge Road, London SW1V 2SA.

Published in Australia by Random House Australia Pty., Level 3, 100 Pacific Highway, North Sydney, NSW 2060.

Copyright © Tony Ross, 1999

The rights of Tony Ross to be identified as the author and illustrator of this work have been
asserted by him in accordance with the Copyright, Designs and Patents Act, 1988.

All rights reserved. Colour separated in Switzerland by Photolitho AG, Zürich.

Printed and bound in Singapore by Tien Wah Press.

10   9   8   7   6   5   4   3   2   1

British Library Cataloguing in Publication Data available.

ISBN 978 1 84270 835 4